The Shteinmekel Tales

Helmut's Secret

By Arielle Fox
(Miss Fox)

Miss Fox Books
New York

This Book is Dedicated with Love to
♡ Ethan, Jack, and Lila ♡
With Special love and thanks to
My Dad Jerry Fox and to Janell!

Hi, my name is Helmut and I wear a helmet too!
It protects my SECRET that I just might share with YOU!
The secret is **nesting** inside of my nose—now that's your

First Clue!

I'll tell you more after you meet my family—
The Shteinmekel Crew!

My Papa   My Mama

Me again!   and my sis,

Yep, that's **My Family** and all of the things that we like to do!

Now it's time to give you clue #2!

Sometimes my secret tweets, sometimes it chirps, and sometimes...
it can even cuckoo!

I see that **YOU**'ve got something special inside of **YOU** aswell.
That's why I've chosen **YOU** to be the kid I am going to tell.

Are you prepared to hear the **TOP** secret that no one else knows?

Okay, get ready, get set, here it goes!

I've got **BIRDS** inside of my **NOSE**!

The teeny tiny birds were once searching for a home that would suit them BEST!
It was <u>inside</u> of our beautiful noses that they chose to rest!

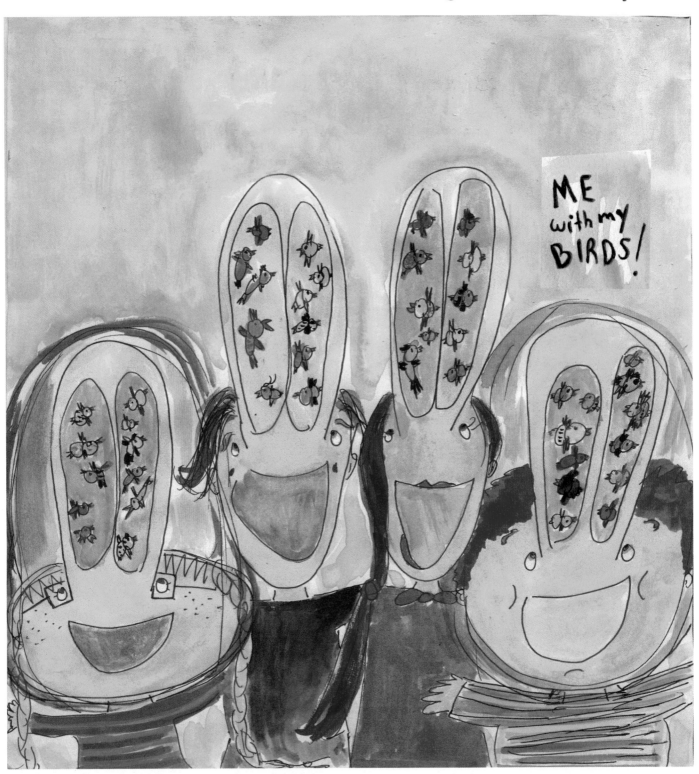

ME with my BIRDS!

Mama invented a SPECIAL MIXTURE for our nostrils—
two drops, one in each side.

It prevents us from feeling the pointy beaks
and claws that are bopping around inside.

Listen closely as each one of our feathered friends sings its own sweet song,
with melodies dear and different, in our noses big and long.

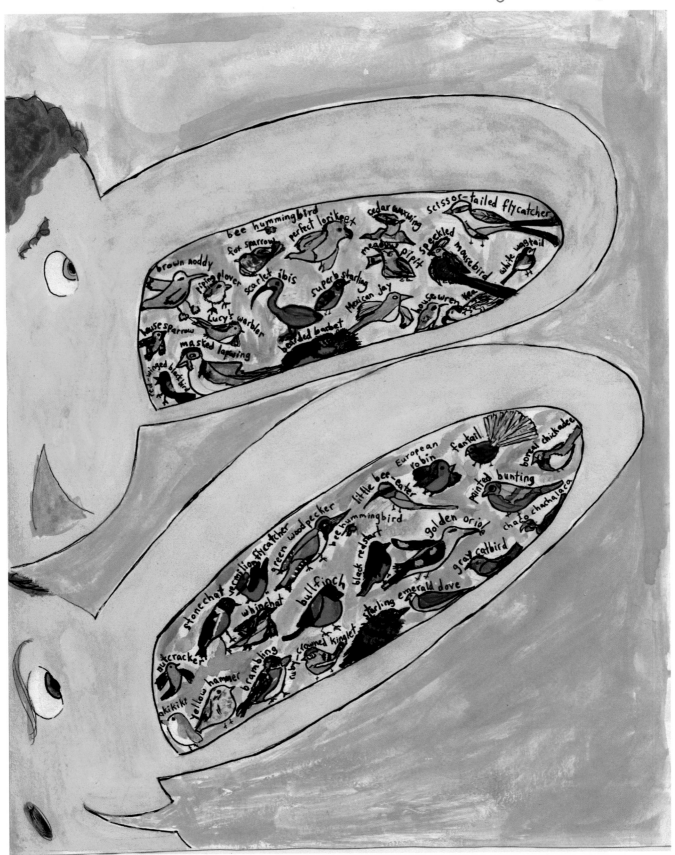

Our Shteinmekel birds—they always get along!

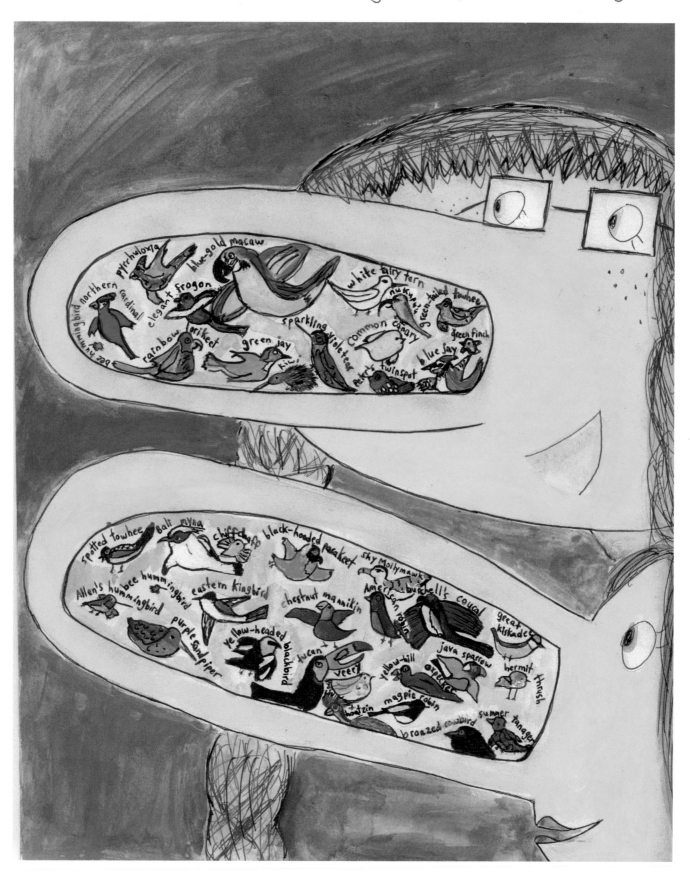

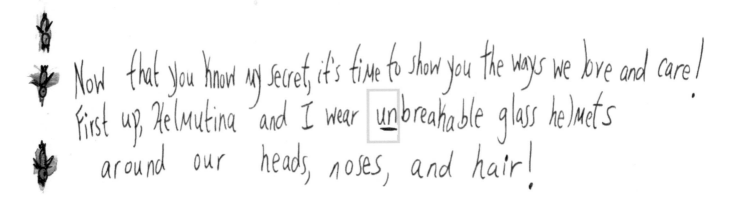

Now that you know my secret, it's time to show you the ways we love and care!
First up, Helmutina and I wear unbreakable glass helmets
around our heads, noses, and hair!

Do you know how children love to run and play?

Well, sometimes we bump our noses, if it's a wild sort of day.
So our helmets protect our birds in the most safe and secure way.

But because Mama and Papa are grown-ups, they do NOT get to play.
So they don't need to wear helmets and their birds are perfectly okay!

And every day, two times per day into the tubs we go!
We must spritz and spray to give the birds—and our noses—
a most stellar clean and healthy glow!

Of course we feed our birds well, with the finest of seed!
While we laugh and tell stories, my jokes always take the lead!

"Why did the little bird hop across the road?
He forgot he was a chicken—he thought he was a toad!"

But now is NOT the time for joking around like a clown.
Things are becoming super serious because we're Moving to a new town.
We're going because of Mama's AWESOME job Opportunity, that she
just canNOT turn down!

As we sail to our new town, we must keep our secret tucked in tight.

That's because when we arrive there, there will be SOMEONE who is quite a fright!

The MAYOR of the newtown SHOUTS just like an angry shark.
His words all over the news are frighteningly dark.

He declares, "It's BEST if everyone is the SAME!"
Since nobody else has birds, keeping ours a secret is my family's biggest aim!

YOU MUST KEEP THE SECERET!!!!
No one may know!!
Don't tell!!
Keep the secerect!
Keep it inside!
Quiet!
Keep it to yourself!
Shhh!
Don't tell!
Keep the Seceret!

Every day Mama and Papa warn me
Not to break our number 1 family rule!
"Don't tell anyone about our secret birds —
especially anyone at your new school!"

So we're training our birds NOT to make a sound.
With the first day of school coming soon,
there's NO Time to fool around!

We're getting ready by polishing our helmets squeaky clean!
I sure do hope that my teacher is nice and that the kids
are NOT MEAN.

Will my birds stay quiet at school **OR** will there be **trouble** waiting for me?
Meet me in Book #2 to find out and see!

I just can't wait to see you
next time on my first day of school!
Meeting <u>YOU</u> sure has been supercool!

<u>Oh</u>! And **PLEASE** don't forget these <u>very</u>
<u>important</u> <u>words</u>:
Do <u>NOT</u> tell anybody about my family's
secret Shteinmekel-birds!

Shhhhhhhhhhhhhhh

About the Author

(A message from the author Miss Fox.)

Hi everyone! I'm Miss Fox. I have been teaching the first grade at a school in Brooklyn, New York for 15 years! One of my favorite parts of the school day has always been reading picture books to my students. So, I finally created my own! When I was a little girl I loved playing make-believe and drawing. These days I still love using my imagination to create characters and to tell stories. So I write, draw, and paint all about the Shteinmekels as much as I can! I hope that you have enjoyed getting to know Helmut, the Shteinmekels, and their birds as much as I have enjoyed sharing it all with you!

Love, Miss Fox

How did the author Meet ♡ The Shteinmekels? ♡

(Another Message from Miss Fox!)

When I was a little girl, my dad Jerry Fox used to tell me stories. He made up The Shteinmekels for me! I never forgot about the one-of-a-kind family and their magical birds. When I became a teenager I started babysitting for children in the small neighborhood in Brooklyn, where I grew up. I began to to tell those children my own Shteinmekel stories! Those children are all grown up now and they still remember the Shteinmekels! Today I am thrilled to create shteinmekel picture book stories to share with you! I hope the Shteinmekels and their birds fly into the hearts of children and readers everywhere, just like they flew into mine so long ago!

? Some THINKING? Questions for YOU!

♡ Hey Readers! Here are some questions to help make story-time even more fun! ♡

1. Which bird is your favorite bird in Helmut's nose?

2. Which bird is your favorite bird in Papa Shteinmekel's nose?

3. Which bird is your favorite in Helmutina's nose?

4. Which bird is your favorite in Mama Shteinmekel's nose?

5. Why are the Shteinmekels keeping their birds a secret?

6. What do you think school will be like for Helmut?

7. Do you think Helmut will be able to keep his family's secret?

8. Besides playing with their birds, what are some things that you think each of the Shteinmekels love to do most?

9. What are some things that you love to do most?

10. What are some things that you might like to do with the Shteinmekels' birds?